I Smell The Future:
A Dog's Story

David Kirk

CALLAWAY & KIRK

New York

Sparky was an extraordinary dog, so it stood to reason that he'd have an extraordinary nose.

Only he didn't. In fact, he couldn't smell the difference between a monkey and a bar of soap, between his master and a barrel of nuts, or between dinner and a stinky rag. For a dog, this was terribly embarrassing, so one morning on his daily walk with Nova, he asked for an upgrade.

"Of course!" said Nova. "I'll give you the best sniffer on the planet. Your nose will be so sensitive," he joked, "you'll be able to smell the future!"

Sparky yipped, wondering at such marvels. He trotted ahead to tell his friends Princess Aerial and 40-Watt dog the news. His master was the best master on Roton!

As Nova wired his new circuits, Sparky dreamed of the wonderful things he would smell. Morning oil would smell sweeter. His master would smell more masterful. He would smell when Cathode the cat was sneaking up behind him to scrape her sharp claws on his rump and take his warm spot. But the best trick of all would be to smell the future!

Sparky slept until morning. Even before he opened his eyes, he knew he was different. Clear pictures appeared in his mind, not of light, shape, or color, but of smell. He smelled the position of every animal in the house.

He smelled the scented oils inside bottles in Nova's mother's room. He could even smell what sorts of spaceships were cruising by outside. But Sparky was eager to test the other wonder Nova had promised. He would smell the future!

He clattered onto Nova's sleep platform, where Cathode was curled on the pillow, and sniffed. "Why are you sniffing?" Cathode demanded.

"I am smelling what you will do next," said Sparky. "With my new upgrade, I can smell the future."

"Ridiculous," mewed Cathode. "No one can predict what a cat will do."

"But it's true," insisted Sparky. "Nova said so."

"You may smell better," sighed Cathode, "but Nova was joking. You cannot smell the future."

"You are a cat," said Sparky, "and know nothing of trust. I *can* smell the future."

To prove his point, Sparky put his nose in the air and sniffed. Suddenly, he knew what would happen next. From the kitchen, there would be the scraping of the can-opener, a pop, some gurgling, and then Nova's mother would call him to breakfast. He sniffed again, now sensing that it was delicious, fresh oil she'd be pouring into his bowl.

"I predict that I am about to have my breakfast," said Sparky, eyeing Cathode defiantly. "Luna will call me."

At that very moment, the scrape, pop, and gurgle that he'd predicted resounded through the house. Luna called his name. Sparky padded to the kitchen and lapped up his breakfast. His prediction had been correct. The oil was delicious!

Raising his nose, a flash of certain knowledge electrified Sparky's brain once again. Nova would take him for a walk! As soon as this thought entered his head, in walked Nova, leash in hand.

As they strolled the dog path, Sparky tested his new abilities, sniffing the air for the scent of the future. *Flash!* He smelled that he would see his friend, 40-Watt dog. Around the bend, 40-Watt appeared as if by magic. *Flash!* Sparky smelled that he would meet Princess Aerial and they would stop for a sniff. Again, his prediction came true!

Sparky told his friends his amazing story. Everyone was awed by his new power— except Cathode.

"Of course Nova's mother gave you oil for breakfast," she mewed. "It's what you get every morning! And every morning Nova takes you on a walk and you see 40-Watt dog and have a sniff with Princess Aerial. You are not fore-smelling the future, you silly dog!"

Sparky shook his head sadly. "I smelled that you would say that," he sighed.

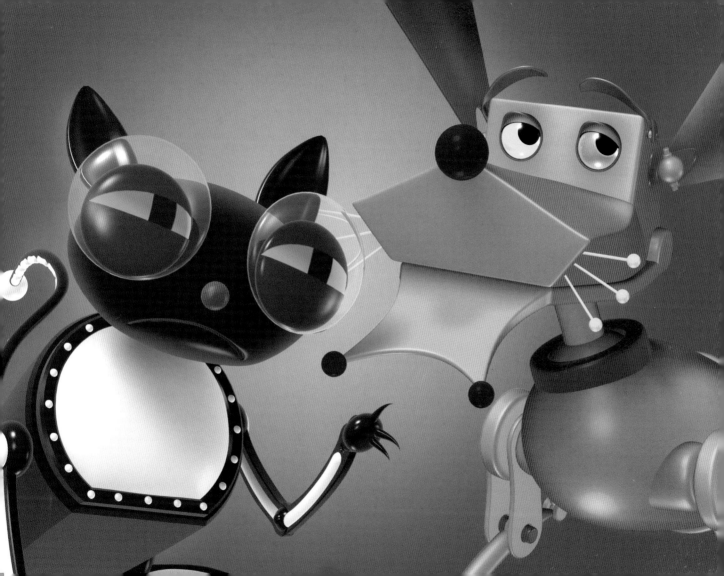

athode considered herself a patient cat, but this sort of nonsense was too much. "Please, oh smeller of the future," she mewed sarcastically, "tell us of tomorrow! What will you have for breakfast? Who will take you for your walk?"

Sparky sniffed and considered. "I will have oil for breakfast," he announced, "and Nova will take me for my walk."

The other animals listened in amazed silence. How did Sparky smell these things?

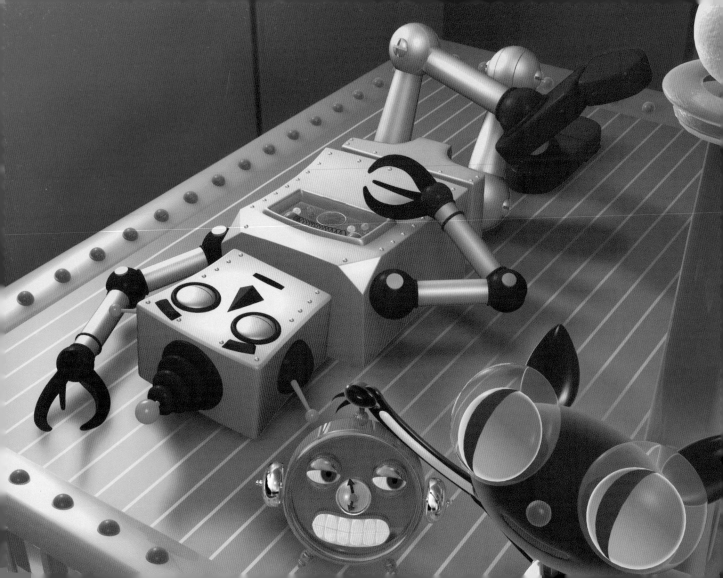

The next morning, Cathode rose before dawn. She stretched, then slinked to the kitchen to hide the can-opener. That accomplished, she crept into Nova's room to turn off his alarm, doing the same in Nova's parents' room.

When Luna called Sparky for breakfast, he was horrified to see his bowl filled not with fresh oil, but with a rusty heap of nuts and bolts.

"Sorry about the leftovers," said Luna. "The can-opener is missing."

Sparky sniffed. His stomach turned uncomfortably. He looked about for Nova. Maybe he'd find some oil to drink on his walk. But Nova was heading out the door with his schoolbag over his shoulder.

"Sorry fella, I'm late for school. Mom's going to walk you."

Luna took Sparky for his walk. He did not see his dear friends Princess Aerial or 40-Watt, but was instead chased by mean dogs. Cathode had been right. He could not smell the future. Nova had not told him the truth.

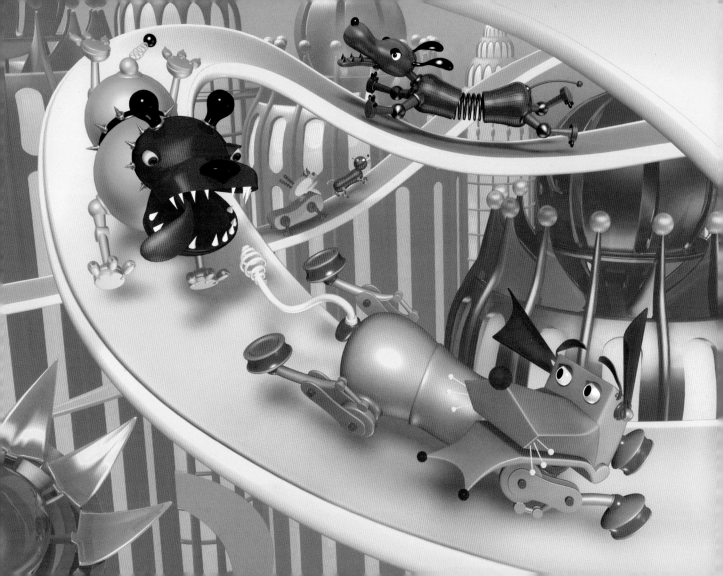

When his master came home after school, Sparky did not run to meet him, but lay with his head on the floor.

As the evening passed, Cathode began to feel bad about what she had done. Being right was no fun when it made a friend miserable.

She went to him. "I hid the can-opener," she said, "and I turned off the alarm clocks, too."

Sparky didn't look up.

"It doesn't matter," he sighed. "Nova said I would smell the future, and I cannot smell the future. What more is there to say?"

Cathode thought for a moment. Suddenly, she knew what needed to be said.

"Actually," she mewed, "you *can* smell the future. But do you suppose that you are the only animal in the house with a talent? Nova gave me the power to *change* the future."

Raising his head, Sparky looked at the cat in astonishment.

"I never knew that," he said. "How is it done?"

"That is my secret," she mewed, "because I am a cat, and a cat may keep secrets. But you will know when I have used my talent for changing the future—when your talent for smelling it has failed you."

Sparky leapt to his feet. "I have to go," he said. "I smell that my master will be waiting for me."

Cathode watched Sparky trot happily to find Nova. Then, purring contentedly, she curled into the warm spot he had left behind.

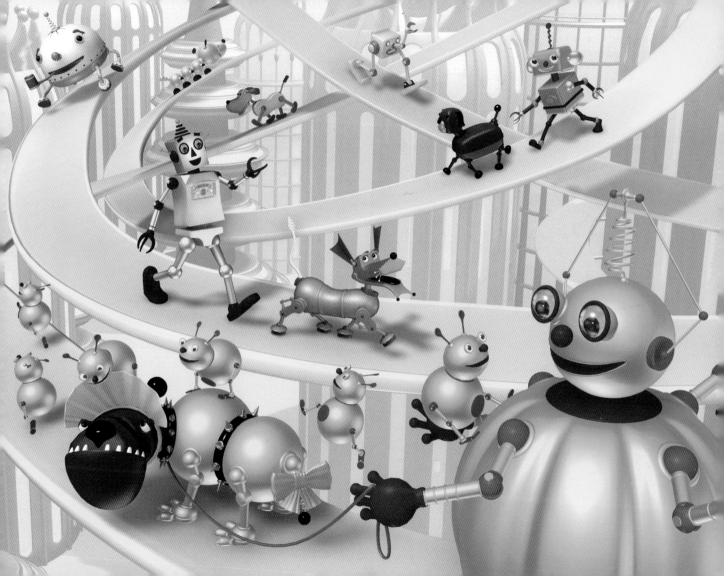

Nicholas Callaway, President and Publisher
Cathy Ferrara, Managing Editor and Production Director
Toshiya Masuda, Art Director • Nelson Gomez, Director of Digital Services
Joya Rajadhyaksha, Associate Editor • Amy Cloud, Associate Editor
Bill Burg, Digital Artist • Keith McMenamy, Digital Artist • Christina Pagano, Digital Artist
Raphael Shea, Senior Designer • Krupa Jhaveri, Designer

Library of Congress Cataloging-in-Publication Data available upon request.

Distributed in the United States by Viking Children's Books.

Callaway Arts & Entertainment, its Callaway logotype, and Callaway & Kirk Company LLC are trademarks.

ISBN 0-448-43995-6

Visit Callaway Arts & Entertainment at www.callaway.com

10 9 8 7 6 5 4 3 2 1   06 07 08 09 10

First edition, October 2006
Printed in China